PATRICIA ST JOHN

The Other Kitten

Illustrated by Gunvor Edwards

Friska my Friend

Illustrated by Toni Goffe

SCRIPTURE UNION

The Other Kitten

Friska my Friend

Scripture Union, 207–209 Queensway, Bletchley, Milton
Keynes, MK2 2EB, England.

ISBN 1 85999 312 5

British Library Cataloguing-in-Publication Data.
A catalogue record of this book is available from the British
Library.

Printed and bound in Great Britain by
Creative Print and Design (Wales), Ebbw Vale.

Scripture Union is an international Christian charity working with
churches in more than 130 countries, providing resources to bring
the good news about Jesus Christ to children, young people and
families and to encourage them to develop spiritually through the
Bible and prayer.

As well as our network of volunteers, staff and associates who run
holidays, church-based events and school Christian groups, we pro-
duce a wide range of publications and support those who use our
resources through training programmes.

Chapter one

Mark woke first and lay, still half asleep, trying to remember. Then he woke properly and it all came back to him. He jumped out of bed, ran to the window, flung it wide open and stuck his head far out.

What a morning! The sun was just rising behind the trees at the bottom of the garden and the dew on the grass sparkled like silver, except for the golden patches where the daffodils grew. The birds were singing wildly, madly. Mark dressed quickly and opened

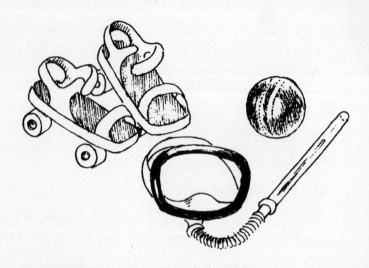

his suitcase to see that nothing had been forgotten. He pushed aside the clothes that Mum had packed and checked the really important things: his roller skates, his anorak, his swimming trunks (he was determined to bathe, however much Gran said it was too cold), his underwater goggles, snorkel and cricket ball. His bat and shrimping net would be strapped to the case and he would carry his football under his arm. Everything was in order.

He thought he had better wake Carol in case she made them late, fussing over her packing. He crossed to her room where she lay asleep, her hair spread all over the pillow, pulled the bedclothes off her and tweaked her toes. She sat up, started to be cross and then remembered too.

'It's today, isn't it?' she said.

'Of course, stupid; you don't think it's yesterday, do you?'

She ran to the window. 'It's a lovely day,' she said. 'I'm going to say goodbye to the rabbits.'

Carol was so sure of her packing that she had strapped it all up the day before, with her spade and bucket on top of the case. She pulled on her jeans and shirt and ran downstairs and into the garden. She picked some dandelion leaves as a farewell present and disappeared round the corner of the house. Mark was left alone.

'I'd better wake Mum and Dad,' he thought. 'We've got to get to Gran's by lunch-time and they take a lot longer to dress than we do.' He decided to take them a cup of tea and made it very carefully, warming the pot and pouring the top of the milk into the jug. When he reached the bedroom, carrying the tray, he kicked the door open with a bang. His parents both opened their eyes, blinked and yawned.

'What on earth do you think you're doing, Mark?' said Dad. 'It's only a quarter past six.'

Mark placed the tray on the bedside table. He poured out three cups and sat down on the rug with his own. 'You said you wanted to start early,' he reminded them. 'I was afraid I might oversleep.'

'I didn't mean this early,' grumbled Dad with another yawn, but they both sat up and drank their tea. It was cosy and still half dark in the bedroom and Mark suddenly wondered if he wanted to go away after all. 'You'll tell us when the baby comes, won't you?' he said. 'I hope it's a boy. Carol's hopeless at cricket.'

Mum laughed. 'It can't be long now,' she said. 'But Carol wants a girl, so someone is going to be disappointed. Dad and I have decided to be pleased with whatever comes. Anyhow, where is Carol?'

'Saying goodbye to the rabbits. Dad, you'd better get up, and you too, Mum. You take such ages dressing. I'll lay breakfast and bring down the luggage.'

Dad grumbled a little but decided that it would not hurt to start early. 'The sooner we go, the sooner I'll come back,' he remarked to Mum as he began shaving.

Mark had breakfast ready long before they had finished upstairs, but they appeared at last and Carol came in from the garden, sniffing and looking sad.

'I'll take great care of your rabbits, Carol,' said Mum, 'so don't worry. There'll be wild rabbits in the field opposite Gran's.'

'And squirrels in the wood,' said Dad.

'And lambs at the farm,' said Carol, cheering up.

'And the old horse who sticks his head over the gate,' said Mark. 'I'm going to ride him this time. Mr Cobbley said I could.'

'And me,' said Carol.

'No, you're too little. Mr Cobbley said so.'

'He didn't.'

'He did.'

'He didn't!'

'Now stop it!' said Mum. 'If you argue like that at Gran's, she'll pack you off home. Mark, you're the eldest; you must promise me . . .'

'OK,' said Mark. 'I'll try; but it's Carol who starts it.'

'I don't then,' said Carol.

'You do then.'

'I don't.'

'STOP IT,' said Dad so loudly that they both stopped at once. They stuffed their mouths with toast and marmalade and gave each other a kick under the table.

'Now let's be off,' said Dad. 'It was a good idea waking us so early, Mark. If we start at once we shall be almost on the motorway before the rush hour.'

They hugged Mum and bundled into the back of the car, leaning out to wave and blow kisses. The streets were still quiet and the shops shut. In a very short time they had left the town behind and were out in the country where the fields were starred with daisies and the trees were bursting into leaf. And, although you could not hear them above the noise of the car, Carol knew that all the birds were singing as they built their nests. She stuck her head out of the window and laughed softly for joy. It was going to be a wonderful holiday.

Chapter two

It was a wonderful journey too, and they did not quarrel once. They played the animal game, seeing who could score a hundred first; one for a sheep, one for a cow, two for a horse, three for a pig, a cat or a dog, and four for a rabbit. Carol even saw a hedgehog, which counted for five.

Later, on the motorway, they felt thirsty so they stopped at a service station and had a can of pop each and an ice cream. Mark chose a Cornetto and Carol a Bigfoot. They

each had a turn on a Space Invader machine
and then raced back to the car. The day was
getting hot by now and the traffic was
heavy. Mark was sorry when they turned
off the M5 because he loved racing the lor-
ries, but Carol was glad. She loved the little
narrow roads that wound up and down,
and the glimpses from the hilltops of baby
lambs in green fields. Then suddenly they
both gave a shout for there was a notice

ahead of them and it said DEVONSHIRE.

'Not long now,' said Dad. 'We'll soon see the tidal river, and then the sea.'

The first glimpse of the sea was always exciting and today it was blue and tossing with little white waves breaking all over it. They turned south and soon the children began to remember the bridge across the river, the steep, steep hill to the cliff top and the wide coast road that climbed and dipped; then the cottages and the village shop, where they turned left into Gran's lane. Two minutes more, and they caught sight of Gran herself standing at the door

to welcome them, and in thirty seconds they were out of the car and Carol had run right into her arms.

'Can I sleep in the little room where the roof comes down to the floor?' whispered Carol.

'Hullo, Gran,' said Mark, pushing Carol aside and giving Gran a kiss. 'Can we go to the sea this afternoon and can I swim?'

Gran looked horrified. 'In April?' she exclaimed. 'I should have thought it was far too cold. What does Daddy say?'

'They're tough,' said Dad. 'Cold water won't hurt them. How are you, Mother? It's good to be here again.'

They carried in the luggage and took it upstairs. Carol had the attic where the roof came down to the floor, and Mark had the room overlooking the sea where he could watch the ships steaming up and down the Bristol Channel. But they had not got long to unpack because lunch was ready. They clattered downstairs to the low stone kitchen, where Granny was serving up fried chicken and chips, followed by trifle.

Dad left soon after lunch and Gran, who would not have minded a rest, got out her car, for the cliff road was long and steep. Mark and Carol flung their bathing things, snorkel, spade and bucket on to the back seat. 'Do we have to go in the car?' asked Mark. 'Can't we run?'

'If you keep to the side of the road, you can,' said Gran. 'But I'm not running, and you'll be glad of the car coming back. Now, off you go!'

They ran and ran, down through the dark woods where the stream ran along beside them below the road, and then out into the sunshine where the cottages began and great drifts of primroses grew on the banks. Gran came behind them, parked the car, and ran with them down the rocky path that led to the beach. They had arrived and the sun was shining and small waves were breaking in foam on the sand.

'Quick,' shouted Mark, flinging off his clothes. 'Where's my snorkel?' He raced for the sea, but Carol was not in quite such a hurry. It was very cold and she did not stay in long. Instead she built an enormous sand-castle with Gran, to try and stop the tide.

'How far does the water come?' asked Carol.

'Right up to the wall,' said Gran, 'and it's coming very fast. Look, there's hardly any sand left. We'll soon have to move the towels and our castle isn't going to last long.'

Mark came in from the sea to help. They shovelled more sand on the back of the castle and put stones in front, but it was no good. It soon crumbled and the sea seemed to be running up the shore. Everyone was packing up and leaving and the children were suddenly glad that they had not got to walk up that steep hill. It had been a long, exciting day and by the time they had reached home and had some tea and watched Blue Peter and visited the horse, they were quite tired. By seven o'clock, Carol's eyes were closing.

'You can't go to bed yet,' said Mark. 'It's much too early.'

'It's the sea air,' said Gran, 'and getting up so early. Suppose you have some supper now and then go up to bed and I'll come and tell you a story.'

'Oo yes,' said Carol. She loved Gran's stories. Mark thought he was rather old for stories in bed, but he did not mind listening to Carol's. He gave a great yawn.

'Think I'll go to bed too,' he said. 'And I

might come in and listen to Carol's story. Is it about smugglers and wreckers?'

Gran laughed. 'No,' she said. 'I'll tell you about them when we go to the wreck museum. Now, come and have your supper.'

Half an hour later Carol had snuggled down in bed and Gran was sitting beside her. Through the open attic window they could see the sky, still bright from the sunset. There was a wind blowing up from the sea and Carol wondered what it would be like on the beach with the dark waves

breaking against the cliff. She gave a little shiver.

'Is it high tide now?' she asked.

'It will just have turned,' answered Gran. 'There'll be plenty of sand tomorrow morning. Shall I tell you a story about a boat and a storm?'

There was a big bounce on the end of the bed as Mark arrived in his pyjamas. 'Me too,' he said, curling up under the blanket. So Gran told them about a dark night, long ago, when the wind came sweeping down from the hills, whipping up the waves and the twelve friends of Jesus were caught in a storm as they tried to row across the lake. They thought their boat was going to sink, and they wished so much that Jesus was with them. But Jesus had stayed behind.

Then suddenly one of them looked up and saw someone coming towards them, walking on the water. At first they were very

frightened and thought it was a ghost. Then they saw that it was Jesus, coming to them.

'I've heard that story before,' said Mark, 'and I don't believe it. No one could walk on the water.'

'Well, we couldn't,' said Gran. 'But if Jesus was really God, then he made the sea and the land. And if you make something, you can do what you like with it.'

'Oh, shut up, Mark,' said Carol. 'Go on, Gran, what happened?'

So Gran went on. 'Peter, one of the friends, saw Jesus and he thought, "I'd rather be with Jesus on the sea than without him in the boat". So he called out, "If it's really you, tell me to come to you."

' "Come," said Jesus, and Peter slipped over the side and he too walked on the water, looking hard at Jesus all the time. But suddenly he looked away and saw the great, black waves. He was very frightened and began to sink. "Lord, save me," he shouted.

'Jesus seized hold of his hand just in time. "Why were you afraid?" he said. "Why didn't you believe in me?"

'They walked back to the boat together. As soon as they got in, the wind stopped. Everything was safe and all right when Jesus was there. And it's still like that today,' said

Gran. 'If Jesus is with us, loving us and looking after us, then everything is safe and happy. But we have to ask him.'

The sky was quite dark now, and two stars were shining in at the window. Carol was nearly asleep. It had been rather a frightening story and she was glad it had ended like that, loved and safe and happy because Jesus was there. She thought of the wind and the waves and the high tide. She wanted always to feel safe and happy too. She would ask Gran to tell her more about Jesus another night.

Chapter three

The next three days passed happily. They stayed on the beach when the sun shone, and if it was dull or rainy they went to the farm and fed a motherless lamb with a bottle. A little late lamb was born one morning and they watched it take its first wobbly steps. Every evening they phoned their mother to ask if the baby had arrived, but it seemed to be taking its time. However, they got news of the rabbits and told Mum and Dad what they were doing. The first night, they had a fight over the receiver and nearly pulled the phone on to the floor, so after that, Gran stood by and timed them, one minute each.

And every night when Carol was tucked in bed, Gran came and told her a story from the Bible. Carol was beginning to think that the Bible was a very interesting book with so many stories about Jesus. He seemed such a kind person, always helping people and making them well and happy; and Gran said that, although they could not see him, he was still there, ready to help anyone who asked him. Mark still said he did not believe it and he would rather have stories about wreckers and smugglers but he always came and listened, curled up at the bottom of the bed and, sometimes, when Gran stopped, he told her to go on.

The time raced by, and it was not till the fourth day that they had their first real

quarrel. They were just finishing breakfast;
Gran was talking to the milkman and they
were alone.

'I'm going to see the horse,' said Mark.
'Tell Gran.'

'You can't,' said Carol, standing in front
of the door. 'It's your turn to dry the dishes.
Gran said we were to help in turns.'

'I did it yesterday,' said Mark. 'Get out
of the way.'

'You didn't,' shouted Carol. 'I did it at supper.'

'Supper doesn't count. It's only a little bit. I did it at dinner so it's your turn.'

'It's not!'

'It is!'

' 'Tisn't then, and I shan't!'

'Neither shan't I. Get out of the way!'

'I shall tell Gran!'

'I don't care. Get out of the way or I'll push you!'

'You can't!'

'I can!' And he did. When Gran came back, they were both on the floor, screaming and punching and scratching. Carol was smaller than Mark, but she could be very fierce.

Gran could be quite fierce too. She pulled them apart and made them stand up. Carol was crying; Mark was sulking.

'He hit me on the head,' sobbed Carol.

'And she bit me,' growled Mark, showing the teeth marks on his arm. 'She's a cry-baby and it's her turn to dry.'

'I'm not and it isn't!'

'You are and it is!'

'STOP IT,' said Gran. 'I'm ashamed of you both. You can both dry and if there's any more of this you can stay apart in your rooms instead of going to the sea, and that would be a great pity, because it's going to be a lovely day.' So they dried up in angry silence, making faces at each other behind Gran's back. When they had finished, she fetched a shopping basket and a list.

'Go down to the shop,' she said, 'and make it up on the way. It's the best day yet and, if you come back smiling and friendly, we'll go to Hartland Point this afternoon and see the lighthouse.'

They set off, walking a long way apart but Gran had been right. It was hard to remember a quarrel on such a bright day when everything was joyful. The birds were twittering excitedly over their nests and the lambs were skipping round their

mothers. Mark ran to catch up Carol and
Carol stopped sniffing. By the time they
reached the shop they were happy again
and planning how to spend their pocket-
money.

There was only one shop in the village
and they had to wait some time to be served.
Mark stood in the queue with the basket,
but Carol wandered outside and looked
round. There was a path behind the shop
leading up to some cottages, and at the top
of the hill was a caravan site. They had
never been up there and Carol thought there
would be a lovely view of the coast. Mark
was sure to be ages; she would run a little
way and see.

But she never got to the top of the hill
because, when she reached the gate of the
first cottage, she saw the notice. She thought
it was the most exciting notice she had ever
seen and she just stood staring and staring.

This is what it said:–

KITTENS GIVEN AWAY FREE TO GOOD HOMES.

'Ours is a good home,' thought Carol. A kitten was almost as much fun as a new baby. She must tell Mark at once. She ran back to the shop and found Mark, having finished his shopping, standing at the door looking for her. She seized his free hand.

'Come quick,' she shouted. 'I've found something lovely.'

'What?'

'Come and see.' She took half the basket and almost dragged him up the hill. When they reached the notice they both stood staring at it.

'Would Gran let us?' asked Mark.

'She'd have to, if we took it back with us,' said Carol. 'Anyhow, we'd take it home soon. Mum wouldn't mind.'

'I think we'd better ask her,' said Mark

slowly. He was determined to go to Hartland Point and he didn't want any more trouble. 'But, of course, we could always go in and look at them.'

'Yes, let's,' said Carol, pushing open the gate and dancing up the path. She knocked loudly at the door and a woman opened it.

'We've come to see the kittens,' said Carol. 'We've got a good home. We're staying with Mrs White; she's our Gran.'

'Come in,' said the woman. 'They're ready to go, and I'll be glad to be rid of them. Your Gran's a friend of mine; she'd know how to look after a kitten. They're all out here in the woodshed.'

Mark and Carol knelt down in the woodshed and forgot all about everything. There were four kittens with long, soft fur and round blue eyes, crawling in and out of the basket or scampering back to their mother for a feed. Carol picked up a grey tabby; Mark picked up a black one with four white paws and a white nose.

'We'll have this one,' he said, 'and I shall call it Tippet because of the white tips on its paws and nose.'

'No,' said Carol, 'we're having this one, and I shall call it Fluff because it's so soft.'

'We're not,' said Mark. 'I'm the eldest so I ought to choose and I've made up my mind. I'll share it with you and you'll soon

get to like it.'

But Carol wanted the grey kitten more than anything else in the world.

'I saw it first!' she shouted. 'I wish I'd come in to see them without you. We're having this one, I say, or we're not having any at all.'

The woman took away the kittens in a hurry. She was afraid the children might have a fight and pull them in half.

'Dear me!' she said. 'I'm not giving you a kitten if you're going to quarrel over it like that. You can go back to your Gran and ask her what she thinks. When you've made up your minds, tell her to come with you. I'll keep them till I hear from you.'

She led the children out into the garden and shut the door on them. Mark gave Carol a kick. 'You see, you've lost them both now,' he said angrily. 'She'll tell Gran we quarrelled and then Gran will say we can't have them. You always spoil everything, Carol.'

'I didn't,' sobbed Carol, kicking back as hard as she could. 'They were *my* kittens and I found them. I hate you! I'm going to run away, so there! And I'll come back and get Fluff all by myself.'

She was off, slamming the gate behind her and away she ran, down the hill. Mark couldn't see which way she went because the trees hid her from view.

Chapter four

Mark waited for a few minutes, just to show Carol that he didn't care if she did run away. Then he walked back to the shop and looked round. He couldn't see her anywhere.

She was probably hiding, but he wished he knew. She might have run very fast and turned the bend in the road that led to the cottage. She might now be telling tales to Gran and Gran would think it was all his fault, and of course it wasn't, not at all! He was the eldest, and the black and white kitten was by far the prettiest; and he did so want to go and see the lighthouse. He sniffed and felt very sorry for himself.

On the other hand, she might have run into the field opposite the shop and be hiding behind the barn. He was quite sure that she would not have run down the twisty little road that led to the sea because she was afraid of the dark woods. When they were not quarrelling, he always held her hand when they ran between the trees. He didn't like them much himself.

He decided to search behind the barn and, if she wasn't there, he would go home and peep through the kitchen door to see if she had arrived first. If she was not there, he would pretend they were playing outside and wait till she turned up. Carol was such a baby. 'Wait till I get her alone,' he muttered. 'I'll teach her! But not till after we've been to the lighthouse.'

But Carol wasn't behind the barn, nor anywhere in the field, although he walked a little way along, peering into the hedge. He did not find her, but he found a hedge-sparrow's nest, beautifully woven from moss with five bright blue eggs in it. It was so beautiful that he almost forgot Carol and waited quite a long time, crouching in the grass, until the sparrow came back. Then he tiptoed away, feeling rather sorry. If only they had not quarrelled, he could have shown Carol that nest. She would have loved it.

He thought he had better go home with the basket and see what was happening. Gran would be wondering where he was, and if he was nice to Carol, they might still go to Hartland Point. He hurried up the road and stuck his nose cautiously round the back door.

It was very quiet in the kitchen. Gran was all alone, doing the ironing. She looked up and smiled. 'At last!' she said. 'I thought you'd got lost and all my shopping with you. Where's Carol?'

'Er . . . she's playing outside. Can we go over to the farm for a bit?'

'Yes, for half an hour. We'll have lunch early and set off to the lighthouse.'

Mark ran to the farm but Carol wasn't there. He was beginning to get very worried indeed. Whatever would Gran say if she hadn't come back by lunch-time? And, anyway, where was she? For the first time he started to feel really bothered, not just about Gran and the lighthouse, but about Carol herself.

He went back to the shop but the shop-keeper hadn't seen her. He stood at the top of the steep, winding road that led down to the sea and felt even more bothered. But she couldn't have run down there all by herself; he was sure she couldn't. But half an hour was up and there was nothing to be done but to go back and tell Gran. He

shuffled into the kitchen.

'Come along,' said Gran, 'lunch is all ready and I've made some nice scones for tea. Where's Carol?'

Mark hung his head. 'I can't find her,' he muttered. 'She ran away. I've looked everywhere for her.'

'She ran away? But you said you were going to the farm. Did she run from the farm?'

'It was before that; she ran away from the shop. I've looked everywhere, honest I have.'

'But you said she was playing outside. Just when did you lose her? Tell me at once, Mark. How long has she been gone?'

Mark burst into tears. He knew from her voice that Gran was frightened and he suddenly felt very frightened too.

'I don't know,' he sobbed. 'She just ran. I couldn't see where she went. We were on the hill behind the shop and she ran behind the trees and when I came down she wasn't there.'

'Well, if she hasn't come home and she isn't at the farm, she must have run down to the sea. It was very naughty of you, Mark, not to tell me sooner. We must drive down at once and look for her, and if she's not there, we must phone the police.'

Gran hurried to the garage and got out the car, calling to the neighbour to look out, in case Carol came back while they were away. Mark jumped in beside her and they drove slowly down the road, looking to left and right. Neither of them said anything at all. The road ended at the little cluster of white cottages and the shop that sold groceries, ice creams, cups of tea and blue china mugs. From there, the rocky footpath led down to the beach.

But there wasn't any beach. The tide had come in and the waves, blue and sparkling, were breaking against the cliff. Gran turned and spoke to a man and his wife who were drinking tea at a table outside the shop.

'We've lost a little girl of eight,' said Gran. 'Did you happen to notice a child by herself?'

The couple looked at each other.

'Why yes,' said the woman, 'about an hour ago when we came up from the beach. Don't you remember, John? A little girl ran past us; pretty little girl she was, with fair, curly hair. I thought her parents were down there. But she can't be there now. The tide's in.'

'And you haven't seen her since?'

'Come to think of it, we haven't. But we were in the shop for a bit so maybe we didn't notice.'

'Thank you.' Gran's voice sounded strange and tight. Mark glanced up at her and noticed that her face had gone quite white and she seemed to have forgotten all about him.

'I suppose she could have run along into the next cove,' said Gran. 'The cliff is further back there and it may not be too late. We must ring the coastguard at once.'

She went back into the shop leaving Mark standing alone in the road that turned into a rocky path, staring out over the sea. Where, oh where was Carol?

Chapter five

Where was Carol?

When she ran away from the garden where the kittens lived, she was so angry that she hardly knew what she was doing. She wanted to run and run and give Mark a big fright. If she didn't come back for a long time, Gran would be very cross with Mark for not looking after her, so she would run for a long way and get really properly lost.

She would run right down to the sea and

hide behind the rocks. Mark would never catch her up with that heavy basket. She was so angry that she hardly noticed the dark woods; she was much too busy thinking about that darling tabby kitten and hating Mark. 'Fluff, Fluff,' she cried to herself, 'I wanted you so badly. If only I'd never shown Mark. If only I'd just gone in alone and got it. I shan't come back, not for a long time. I hate him.'

She ran right through the dark woods and came out into the sunshine, and the clumps of primroses on the banks were like great yellow pools. She stopped to smell them and

noticed some white violets sheltering under a fern. She smelt them too, but she did not pick them, because she was not going home for a long, long time and they might die.

But she felt better out there in the sunshine and, by the time she had reached the cottages and looked down the path that led to the sea, she had almost decided to go home for lunch. But she still had plenty of time; she would hide for a little in case Mark came to look for her.

She would not go down to the beach because the tide was quite high and all the people were coming up, but there was a little path that ran along the bottom of the cliff for quite a long way. It seemed to turn a corner further on and Mark would never think of looking for her there.

It was fun running along that path on that bright April morning. There were seagulls nesting on the cliff and she watched the

swoop of their white wings and almost forgot her troubles. She felt rather sorry. If only they hadn't quarrelled, she could have shown Mark the gulls' nests. He would have loved them.

The path had turned a corner and she suddenly found herself in another little cove where the cliffs were much further back. Here there was plenty of room and lots of sand and the water seemed quite far away.

She had never been here before and she felt quite excited. She would bring Mark here as soon as they had made up their quarrel. She thought it was even nicer than their own beach and she began to look for shells. There were little pools in the rocks too, with sea anemones waving their tendrils at her and tiny crabs scuttling to and fro. It was so warm and quiet and sheltered that she felt almost sleepy. She had no idea how late it was getting.

It was only when she happened to look up that she noticed how much nearer the water had come and she felt a little bit frightened. It must be nearly lunch-time, she thought, and she still had to climb that steep hill home. She suddenly wanted to get back as quickly as possible. Mark had had plenty of time to have had a big, big fright and Gran had had plenty of time to have been very cross with him. She began to wonder whether Gran might not be rather cross with her too.

She ran to the place where the path had turned the corner and then she forgot all about Mark and Gran and everything else and just stood staring and staring. For there ahead of her was nothing but water. The path was quite covered all the way to the bottom of the cliff and their beach wasn't there any more. The tide had come in and there was nothing at all but sparkling blue

water and little white waves breaking against the rocks.

Carol felt very frightened; she began to cry. She wondered if the sea would come right up to the cliffs in the new cove, because if so, she would be drowned. She couldn't get out either side. She tried to find a path up the cliff, but the rocks were too steep for a little girl to climb. She sat down on a big rock and she had never felt so lonely and afraid before.

She knew that, if she waited long enough, the tide would turn and the path would be there again, but she did not know how far the water would reach in the cove where she was sitting. It was getting nearer and nearer, quite close to her sandals. She thought of her mother and father and the new baby and the rabbits, but they were far away and they couldn't help her. She thought of Gran and Mark. They would be out looking for her now, but how would they know where to look? She wanted Mark to come so badly; Mark would know what to do. She always felt safe when Mark was there. But how could he come when the path was covered with water?

Gran and Mark; she began to think about the cottage: the warm kitchen, the apple blossom in the garden and that cosy time, just before she went to sleep, when Gran sat on her bed telling stories and Mark curled up under the blanket in his pyjamas. She remembered the first story and she began to think about it. It was about the sea, not on a blue sparkly day like this, but on a dark night and there were twelve men who were very frightened, just like she

was. But Jesus had come, walking on the water and they hadn't been frightened any more. Everything was all right when Jesus came.

She remembered something else too. Gran had said that Jesus was still here, although we couldn't see him, and he loved us and listened to us and wanted to help us. Mark said he didn't believe it, but Gran had said it was true and Gran knew more than Mark. Suppose she told him that she needed to be rescued and suppose he came to her, walking on the water? She didn't think he would, but at least she could try.

'Jesus,' she said, closing her eyes and folding her hands because that was what Granny did when she prayed, 'please come and help me. Don't let the water come right to where I am. Please help me to get out.'

She opened her eyes but she was still alone. She began to think about Jesus. Gran had said that he was very good and he wanted us to be good too. But she had quarrelled and kicked and been horrid to Mark. She shut her eyes again.

'Please help me,' she said. 'I won't quarrel any more, ever, and, if you like, I'll let Mark have the black and white kitten.'

She opened her eyes again and blinked; a boat was coming, very fast, round the curve of the cliff. It was coming straight into the cove and she could hear the chug-chug of its engine. For a moment she thought it must be Jesus, but then she remembered that Jesus didn't come in motor boats, he walked on the water. Well, it didn't much matter who it was, as long as they were coming. She jumped up, ran to the edge of the water and shouted and waved with all her might.

The coastguard beached quite close to her. He jumped out and lifted her into the boat. 'Now, what's all this about?' he said, as he pushed off. 'Scaring your Gran and your brother out of their wits, you are. Don't you ever run off by yourself like that again!'

And Carol, holding tight to the side of the boat as it skimmed out of the cove, made up her mind that she never, never would.

Chapter six

Gran and Mark sat on a big rock, just above the water line, waiting for the coastguard to come back. He had arrived very quickly after they had phoned him and he had agreed that it was quite possible that Carol had strayed into the next cove before the tide was right up. But, he had said, that cove would soon be covered as well and he'd better look sharp and get going. He had started the engine and shot off round the corner.

Gran did not speak at all. She seemed to

have forgotten about Mark, sitting so quietly beside her, and he felt terribly lonely. He knew now that, if anything bad had happened to Carol, it was all his fault. Perhaps Gran was very angry with him and that was why she did not speak to him. He looked up at her and saw that her eyes were shut like when she prayed at night, and he knew that she was praying for Carol.

'I wonder if it does any good,' thought Mark. He shut his eyes and began saying quietly to himself, 'Please, God, if you're there, find Carol.'

He started thinking about Carol. What if she never came back? It would be awful without Carol and whatever would Mum and Dad say? He suddenly felt very sorry that he had kicked her and been selfish. 'If Carol comes back,' he said to himself, 'I'll be really nice to her. I'll even let her have the tabby kitten.'

Then he looked up and saw the boat swing round the curve in the coastline, much sooner than they had expected. Mark gave Gran such a push that she nearly fell sideways off the rock. 'Gran,' he yelled jumping up, 'it's coming. Look! Can you see her?'

They stood together shading their eyes against the sun and suddenly Gran gave a great sigh and sat down.

'She's there,' she said. 'Thank God!'

Mark rushed to the entrance of the little bay where the waves lapped against the wall. The coastguard drew in, waved cheerily to Gran and hoisted Carol on to the steps. She and Mark stood with the water right over their sandals and hugged each other. Then Carol ran to Gran. 'Gran,' she said in a surprised voice, 'why are you crying? Can't you see I'm safe?'

'Yes, I can,' said Gran, holding her tight. 'That's why I'm crying.' And then they all started laughing instead.

They were all rather quiet driving back up the hill. Mark and Carol knew that they had both been very naughty and if Gran was going to be cross they really could not blame her. But Gran was not cross. She just seemed very tired.

'We've all had such an awful fright,' thought Gran. 'Let's all be happy now. Perhaps we will talk about it another time,

or perhaps they have learned their lesson without any talking.'

It was too late to go to Hartland Point, so they decided to go next day. But they all enjoyed their lunch and when they had finished Carol was so tired that she fell asleep in the armchair. Then they went to the farm and fed the calves and both had a ride on the horse; and Mark did not say that Carol was too little. He helped her on and off and held the reins so that the horse would not trot too fast.

They went to bed tired but happy and when Gran came for the goodnight story, both Mark and Carol felt that it would be a special sort of story and both listened hard. It was about ten men and they all had a terrible illness called leprosy.

'People still get it,' said Mark. 'In Africa.'

'Yes,' said Gran, 'but now it can be cured. There was no medicine for it then. They became covered with spots and sores and they had to leave their homes and towns in case anyone else caught it. They had to live out on the hills and no one would go near them. Their families would leave food for them to pick up. But these ten men heard about Jesus and they came and stood waiting for him on the hillside. They didn't dare come too near the road. When they saw Jesus coming they all started shouting at the tops of their voices, "Jesus, Master, have mercy on us."

'Jesus stopped. He was not afraid of leprosy. He just wanted to help the men. He told them to go back to their homes because he knew that, by the time they got there, they would all be well.

'And they believed him; they all started rushing down the road shouting for joy and, as they ran, their illness was healed. Their spots and sores disappeared. They were going home strong and well.

'All except one! He suddenly stopped. He was a stranger from another country. Then he turned round and came running back to Jesus and fell down in front of him and began to thank him with all his heart.

'Jesus was rather sad. "I healed ten," he said. "Where are the other nine? Has only one stopped to say thank you?"

'But he was glad about the one. "You can stand up and go in peace," said Jesus. "Your faith has made you well."

'And the tenth man went home much happier than the others. The others had been healed, but the tenth had talked to Jesus and come to know him; and he had made Jesus glad by saying thank you.'

'Shall we say thank you because I was rescued?' asked Carol. 'You know, Gran, when I was there in that cove, I remembered about Jesus walking on the water and I asked him to help me, and then I saw the boat.'

'It wasn't Jesus, it was the coastguard,' said Mark.

'But that's how God answers our prayers,' said Gran. 'Jesus isn't walking about on Earth any more but his love and power are still there, working through other people. It was God who made those people outside the shop notice where you had gone, and who made the coastguard come so quickly. It was God who helped you to sit still and wait quietly instead of trying to climb the cliff or swim along the edge, or anything silly like that. We were praying and he was helping us all the time, and we must certainly thank him.'

So they all shut their eyes and Gran thanked God for looking after Carol and keeping her safe. Carol remembered that terrible moment when she knew that the water was all round her and Gran and Mark remembered how they had sat on that rock and wondered if Carol had drowned. But it had all come right in the end. Even Mark knew that someone had been there, listening to them and helping them.

And Mark and Carol both remembered something else. Since coming home from the beach, no one had talked about the kittens at all. Those kittens needed an awful lot of thinking about.

Chapter seven

Next morning Mark found the sun pouring in through his bedroom window. It was a perfect day for Hartland Point and he jumped out of bed.

'Gran,' he shouted, 'let's have breakfast soon and let's take a picnic to the lighthouse.'

Gran was in the kitchen in her dressing-gown, making herself a cup of tea and she promised to get going early.

'I could go to the shop by myself this

morning,' said Mark, 'and Carol could help you get ready. It would be quicker that way. And can we have crisps and pop with our picnic, Gran?'

'Why yes,' said Gran, 'and, as a great treat, we might finish up with a cream tea at a farm near there. But Carol likes going to the shop too, so we must wait and see what she wants.'

To Gran's surprise, Carol seemed quite pleased with the idea of Mark going shopping alone. In fact, she seemed in quite a hurry to get him out of the house and, as soon as he had left, she pulled Gran down on the sofa beside her.

'Gran,' she said. 'It's about those kittens.'

'What kittens?' asked Gran.

'The kittens we had a fight about,' said Carol. 'We didn't tell you, but that's why I ran away. They're in the house up the hill behind the shop and they're free; you don't have to pay anything, and I wanted the tabby – he's so sweet, Gran, the sweetest little kitten you ever saw. But Mark wanted the black one and we had a big quarrel and I ran away, and then . . .'

Carol was suddenly quiet.

'Well?' said Gran. 'Go on.'

'Well, when I was on the beach,' said Carol very slowly, 'I just thought I didn't want to quarrel with Mark any more, and I thought I'd let him have the black and white kitten after all. And Gran, could we go and get it now, at once, and could we go across the field so we shan't meet him? You see, I want it to be a surprise.

'But,' said Gran, 'what will Mummy say? Does she want a kitten as well as a new baby?'

'She won't mind,' said Carol. 'There's lots of room for both at home. And if she really says we can't have it, you could keep it, Gran and we'd play with it when we come to stay.'

'Well,' said Gran, 'I wouldn't mind. I thought I heard a mouse in the store-room the other day and I did think about getting a cat. Let's go at once, before Mark gets back.'

They found a basket with a lid and went out through the back gate and crossed the field. It was a longer way but much prettier. The dew still lay on the grass, silver and

shining, but the daisies and dandelions were beginning to open their faces to the sunshine. Carol walked rather slowly and she did not say anything at all. It was going to be very hard to see that tabby kitten again and then leave it behind. As they came near to the cottage she took Gran's hand and held it tight.

The woman who had showed them the kittens the day before had gone out, but her husband opened the door. He was pleased to see Gran.

'Come for a kitten, have you? he said. 'The wife told me about your two young'uns yesterday. Made up your mind now, have you? We're in luck this morning. A lad came in not long ago and took one, just after the wife left for market . . .'

Carol gasped. Supposing someone had taken the black and white one and she couldn't give Mark a surprise after all! She ran into the woodshed. It was all right; the black and white one was still there, clawing over the side of the basket. It was the tabby which had gone and Carol was glad. It would have been hard to see it and then to leave it behind.

She held Tippet in her arms. He was very soft and fluffy and looked up at her with big, baby blue eyes. She stroked him softly. 'Dear, dear little Tippet,' she whispered. 'You are not quite as nice as Fluff but I love you very much.' Then she seized Gran's hand. 'Gran, come quick,' she cried. 'I want to show Mark. He'll be home by now.'

They hurried home up the road, carrying the kitten hidden in the basket. When they reached the cottage, Mark was hanging over the gate, looking very pleased with himself.

'Where have you been?' he said. 'I've been looking everywhere for you. You'd better come into the kitchen 'cos I've got a surprise for you.'

'So have I for you,' shouted Carol. She rushed into the kitchen and there, in the middle of the table, was the tabby kitten lapping milk out of Gran's best china saucer.

'It's Fluff,' screamed Carol, 'and here's Tippet.' She opened the basket and Tippet leapt out and tried to push Fluff away from the milk. They both jumped into the saucer and the milk went all over the tablecloth. The kittens stuck their tails in the air and lapped it up.

'For goodness sake, put them on the floor,' said Gran who thought, for a moment, that she was seeing double. 'And get that cloth in to soak. And they can't drink out of my best tea service either. Look, there's a tin plate over on the sink and until they are house-trained, they must sleep in the shed. I don't know what Mummy is going to say about it all. We'll phone her tonight.'

'Can we take the kittens on the picnic?' said Mark.

'We couldn't leave them behind,' said Carol.

So when they had made the sandwiches and packed the picnic and the bathing things, they all set off; Gran driving in front and Mark, Carol, Tippet and Fluff at the back. The kittens travelled in a big cardboard box lined with an old woolly pullover of Gran's. They snuggled down and looked very warm and comfortable and when they reached the lighthouse and had lunch, they ran about in the daisies. In the afternoon, they went on to a little beach and Mark and Carol bathed. Gran sat on a rock and the kittens rolled in the sand. They all finished with a cream team at a farm; it was a beautiful day.

And, all the time, Mark felt loving to Carol because she had given him Tippet and Carol felt loving to Mark because he had given her Fluff. And because they were loving, they were happy; and that was why it was such a beautiful day.

Chapter eight

They phoned Mum that evening at six o'clock. Gran spoke first and Mark and Carol jiggled up and down in the doorway. Of course they could only hear what was being said at one end of the phone, but they more or less knew what was happening by listening to Gran.

'How are things going, dear?' asked Gran. 'Not long? . . . Good . . . Oh, they're fine but they wanted me to ask you something. Would you mind if they each brought home a kitten? . . . Well yes, I know and I'm sorry, but it was a mistake; they each got one for the other . . . Yes, it was meant to be only one; it was all a mistake. I'll write and explain . . . No, there won't be lots more; they are both males . . . Yes, dear, I do realise there's going to be a baby, but it would be safer on the verandah; there are other cats besides these . . . Yes, I know it's all an extra expense but I'll contribute to the cat food . . . Well, just think it over dear, and let us know . . . I'll pass you over to Mark.'

Mark seized the receiver and Carol listened anxiously.

'Mum, it will be all right about the baby,' he said, very fast and loud. 'I had a friend at school and they had a baby and a pram and a cat and they put a net over it . . . It would be much safer because the Browns next door have a huge cat . . . OK, Mum

ask Dad, and tell us tomorrow, but please say yes...'

Carol snatched the receiver from him. 'Mum,' she squealed, 'they're the sweetest little kittens you ever saw, their names are Fluff and Tippet. And Mum, there was only going to be one and we quarrelled, and I ran away and the tide came up and I was nearly drowned and the coastguard rescued me and then we both went and got the other one by mistake... No Mummy, it's all right, I didn't drown at all. I'm quite all right . . . I was just telling you . . .'

Gran took the receiver firmly from Carol.

'Carol's fine,' she said, 'and I'll write and tell you all about it. Just let us know at once if the baby comes. Bye now and God bless. We'll phone tomorrow at six.'

But they didn't phone at six because Dad phoned them at five, and it wasn't about kittens. When they heard the phone ring Mark and Carol went on eating their tea because they thought it was too early for a call from home. Only when they heard what Gran was saying did they run out into the passage and start to clap softly.

'A little boy!' cried Gran. 'Oh, Brian, I'm so very thankful . . . after Grandpa? How lovely! Is Anne all right? . . . Splendid. . . . Yes, I'll have them all ready by lunch-time. They'll be wild to get home. Here they are.'

'It's a boy,' whispered Mark. 'Hurrah!'

'It's a baby,' thought Carol, 'and I don't care if it's a boy or a girl, Mum said I could bath it and take it out in the pram.'

Dad told them both, all over again, about Richard John, called after Grandpa, who weighed nine pounds three ounces and had lots of dark hair and a very loud voice, and when Dad had finished, Carol said, 'And what about the kittens? Can we have them?'

'Kittens?' said Dad. 'What kittens?'

'Our kittens, Fluff and Tippet. Did Mum forget to tell you?'

'Well, she was rather busy thinking about the baby last night. What about them?'

'Well, can we have them? One each.'

'Oh sure, if you'll look after them. A couple of kittens shouldn't be too much trouble. Have them ready in a box when I come on Friday.'

'Friday!' cried Carol, jumping up and down. 'That's the day after tomorrow. Couldn't we go tomorrow, Gran? I just can't wait to see the baby.'

Mark looked thoughtful. He went to Gran and rubbed his head against her shoulder. 'It's not that we want to leave you, Gran,' he said. 'We've had a really good time. It's just that we're longing to see the baby. Couldn't you come with us?'

Gran rumpled his hair. 'It's all right, Mark,' she said. 'I understand. I'm longing to see the baby too, but Auntie's quite close and she'll give a hand. I was hoping you might all come and stay in the summer holidays. That's less than three months away.'

The children thought that this was a lovely plan and, after all, the time went quickly. They went into Bideford next morning and bought presents for the baby with their pocket money; a bib with a robin on it and a pink rattle with a bell inside.

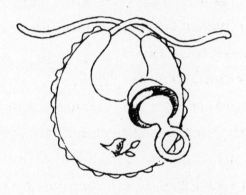

In the afternoon, they had a last swim, and then it was time to pick primroses for Mum, say goodbye to the farmer and the animals, to pack and watch the kittens have their supper. Then, at last, Carol was safe in bed and Mark was sitting cross-legged at the other end with the blanket round him. Gran leaned back in the armchair. She looked quite tired.

'Tomorrow,' said Carol, wriggling her toes, 'I shall be holding the baby.'

'And me,' said Mark. 'You've got to take turns.'

'He's a very lucky baby,' said Gran quickly, before an argument could start, 'to be born into a family like yours, with a loving mother and father, a sister old enough to look after him and a brother old enough to teach him and protect him.'

'And two kittens,' said Carol.

'And four rabbits,' said Mark.

'And all our toys,' said Carol. 'Oh, I just can't wait! Gran, tell us a story, a special one because it's our last night.'

'Very well,' said Gran. 'We've been talking about the baby born into your family, so I'll tell you about a man who wanted to be born again.'

'How silly,' said Mark.

'You couldn't,' said Carol.

'Wait and see,' said Gran.

She told them how the religious leaders of the country where Jesus lived became very jealous of Jesus. Jesus was healing ill people and making the blind see and of course everyone loved him and followed him and no one listened to the ordinary teachers at all. Everyone wanted Jesus.

So the leaders and teachers got together and they made a plan. They told the people that Jesus was a wicked man and they must not go to him or listen to him. But one leader, called Nicodemus, wanted to listen. He knew that Jesus was good and loving but he was afraid to be seen visiting him. So he waited till it was quite dark and then

he crept along the streets and knocked at the door.

'Come in,' said Jesus.

'Master,' said Nicodemus, 'I know that God has sent you, and I want to know how you do all these wonderful things.'

Jesus said to him, 'If you want to understand, you must be born again.'

'That's silly,' said Mark. 'I said so before.'

'What did he mean?' said Carol.

'That's just what Nicodemus wanted to know,' said Gran. 'He was like Mark. We've

94

been talking about your baby, born into your family, belonging to Mum and Dad. Jesus is God's Son and when we come to him and love him, then we become God's children too, and God becomes our heavenly Father. We are born into God's family and all the other people who love Jesus are like our brothers and sisters and we all love and help each other.'

'How?' asked Carol.

'Just by asking,' said Gran. 'Tell God you want to belong to him and call him your heavenly Father. Tell him you want to live his way and love like Jesus loved. Then he will make you part of his family.'

They talked for a little longer and Gran prayed. She thanked God for the new baby and asked that Mark and Carol would understand what it meant to be born into God's family. Then she tucked up Carol and kissed them both goodnight. 'Go to sleep quickly,' she said, 'and then it will be tomorrow.'

Mark went to his room. He knelt at his window with his arms on the sill, and looked out at the black Channel and the great dark sky above it, with stars shining, millions of miles away. It was so big and wide that it made him feel rather small and lonely. Perhaps it would be good to know that he belonged to a heavenly Father who guided the stars and the sea, but who still cared about one boy.

Carol snuggled down under the blankets and thought about the baby: 'Our family . . . God's family . . . Mum and Dad, Mark and me and Richard John . . . Fluff, Tippet and the rabbits and a loving heavenly Father . . . it was nice to belong . . .'

Carol was asleep.

Friska my Friend

Chapter one

Half past three, and on that warm, sunny afternoon in early summer, the children were glad to get out of school. They ran across the playground, pushing and jostling out through the gate. Some jumped into waiting cars but most of them turned down the road that led to the village. Colin went with them, but where the road divided he stopped and his friend Bill stopped too.

'Here,' said Bill, fishing in his satchel, 'I've got something for her. My mum said I could have the leftovers.' And he pushed a greasy paper bag into Colin's hand.

'Thanks,' said Colin. 'Coming to see her?'

Bill shook his head.

'Not now; we're going down to Gran's to tea and Mum said I was to come straight home. Maybe I'll come tomorrow. But, Col, my dad said we've got to do something or tell someone. We can't just keep on giving her things. What'll happen when we go to camp?'

Colin stuffed the greasy bag into his satchel with his school books and nodded. 'I'll tell my dad tonight,' he said. 'He'll know what to do. I wish . . . oh, I do wish . . .'

'Whatcher wish?'

'That I could have her,' said Colin. 'I just wish that she was mine. I'd soon fatten her up.'

Bill nodded. 'I might bring a sausage from Gran's,' he said comfortingly. 'She always has 'em! Bye, Col, see you.' He ran off down the road, and Colin crossed to the lane that led up the hillside toward his home. He was quite glad to be alone because he had a lot to think about. It was a beautiful day and late bluebells and buttercups grew along the hedge. The sun shone warm on his face and from somewhere in the oakwood a cuckoo called. After a time, he turned off the lane and climbed a little track that led to the common beyond. On the edge of the common was a cottage surrounded by a garden.

The garden gate was broken and the paint was cracked. Colin rested his chin on it and looked round. The garden was choked with weeds and the grass had grown as high as his knees. The windows of the cottage were dirty and tight shut. Colin gave a soft whistle.

Nothing happened.

Colin whistled quite loudly with his eye on the window.

There was a sudden rush, and a black dog, half Labrador and half terrier, came streaking round the side of the house barking excitedly. She put her paws on the bottom bars of the gate and pushed her nose through the gap, while her whole thin body quivered with excitement. Colin pulled two greasy bags out of his satchel and fed the dog with half a pasty, some broken bread and biscuits and a cold potato. He stuck his hand through the bars and stroked the

thin flanks. He could count every rib. The
dog nosed his face, licked his cheeks and
whined with pleasure.

'Don't go,' she seemed to be saying.
'Please don't go. I need you so much.'

Colin stayed quite a long time, stroking
and patting the dog and talking to her softly
because she seemed to understand. 'I'm
going to talk to my Dad about you,' said
Colin. 'I'm going to do something. I wish

9

you were mine, I'd soon fatten you up and you'd be the best dog in the village. But I don't suppose Dad would let me; we've got Growler already on the farm.'

He left at last, turning back and waving at the twitching black nose poked through the bars, until the track turned into the wood and he could no longer hear the short, sharp litle barks. He felt very unhappy even though he had promised to go back tomorrow. He did not yet know who lived in that cottage, but he did know that someone was starving that dog. He hurried up the lane and into the farmyard at the top of the hill; he was home.

He liked living at the top of the hill. If you looked behind you, you could see the north end of the hills rising steeply behind his school. On the other side the meadows sloped gently to the woods and hop fields and blossoming orchards of Worcestershire.

It was like being on top of the world, thought Colin, as he trotted across the yard. He went straight to the milking shed because he was quite late and Dad would be busy with the cows. He pushed past the orderly herd who stood waiting their turn outside, and went in.

His father, in his white coat, was fastening the nozzle on the udders of the cows. The electric syphon was whining and the milk was sloshing in the tank. The cows mooed contentedly; it was quite noisy.

'Dad,' shouted Colin, standing on tiptoe, 'there's a dog and she's very thin . . .'

'What's that?' asked Dad stooping down. 'The dog's all right; I've just fed him. Run in and tell Mum I'll be along in about half an hour.'

Colin sighed; it was no good trying to talk to Dad during the milking. Perhaps Mum would help him. He ran over to the house and found Mum putting a big potato pie in the oven. His sister, Joy, had just come in from her school.

'Mum,' said Colin, 'there's a poor dog and she's very, very thin. She might be starving.'

'Then we'd best call the RSPCA. Who does she belong to, Colin?'

'I don't know; it's a cottage and it looks all shut up. What's the RSP something?'

'It's a society that cares for animals that have been badly treated. If she's starving, they'll come and take her. Go and change, Colin, and then you can collect the eggs.'

About half an hour later they all sat down to their tea and Colin started again. 'Dad, there's a dog, and she's very thin, almost starving. How do I get the RS something?'

'Well, you'd best find out who she belongs to first. Where did you see her?'

'Bill and I went up the common to look for nests last week. There's a cottage at the edge of the common and it's all untidy and shut up and the dog's ever so thin.'

His father looked interested. 'That'll be old Charlie's cottage,' he said. 'He went to live there after his wife died. Strange old man, they say he is, and won't let anyone into his house, but that dog was his best friend. Old Charlie would never mistreat his dog; there must be something wrong. Why didn't you tell us before?'

'It was a sort of secret and we thought we'd feed her ourselves. Then we suddenly thought, maybe there's no one there and we'd best tell.'

'Perhaps old Charlie's ill or something,' said Mum. 'Someone ought to call in, or maybe we'd better call the police.'

'Well, he might not like that,' said Dad. 'How about Vicar? You go and tell Vicar, Colin, and ask him to call.'

Colin glanced out at the sloping shadows and the bright sky. It was still quite a long time to sunset. 'I'll go now,' he said.

Chapter two

Colin liked the vicar. He and Joy and Mum
and Dad all went down to the Family
Service on Sundays and Colin went to Boys'
Club on Wednesdays. The vicar was good
fun; he sometimes came to school assembly
and would help with almost anything. Colin
ran all the way to the main road and met
Mr Dixon the vicar, at the corner. He'd been
visiting poor old Mrs Brown who couldn't
get out of her wheelchair.

'Hi, Colin,' said the vicar, 'where you off to?'

'To you,' said Colin, falling against him because he had been running very fast. 'Dad said I was to tell you . . . there's a dog, and she's ever so thin . . . I think she's starving . . . and the house looks all shut up. Bill and I were feeding her but we're going to camp at half term.'

'Who does this dog belong to?' asked the vicar. 'And where is he?'

'It's a she, and Dad says she belongs to ol' Charlie,' said Colin, 'and Dad says you'd best call.'

'Old Charlie?' said the vicar. 'I know him but he doesn't like being called on; never let me into the house. However, let's go and have a look.'

Colin and Mr Dixon climbed the steep lane and turned up the track. It was getting dark in the oak wood and Colin was glad he was not alone. It would soon be sunset but there were no lights in the cottage windows. They stood at the gate and whistled and the dog came rushing out whining and thrusting her nose through the gate. When the vicar pushed it open she jumped up barking. But she knew Colin and when he got hold of her she quietened down and wagged her tail.

'Feel her ribs,' said Colin, stroking her gently.

The vicar knocked on the front door; there was no answer. He went round to the back. There was a pile of bricks against a rain barrel and the dog jumped up and started drinking.

'At least she's had water,' said Mr Dixon. He knocked at the back door and tried the lock. He peered in through the windows. 'I don't think there's anyone here,' he said. 'He must have gone away. We'd better phone up the police and ask them to look into it. In the mean time . . .'

'I'll look after her,' said Colin.

'It would be best to take her home,' said Mr Dixon. 'Would your dad mind?'

'I don't think so,' said Colin.

'Well, I'm sure we can sort her out in a day or two,' said the vicar. 'She'll just be a lodger.'

'Not if I can help it,' said Colin. 'If anything's happened to ol' Charlie, I'm keeping her. She's mine.'

'Well, we'll see,' said the vicar. 'Take her home now and give her a good supper. Tell your dad I'll look after old Charlie. 'Bye, Colin, and thanks.'

'Thanks a lot,' called Colin. He kept tight
hold of the dog's collar but she didn't
struggle. She seemed glad to follow her new
master. They climbed the hill together and
when they reached the top the sun was set-
ting and the farm and the barns stood black
against a crimson sky. They reached the
house and Colin pushed open the door. The
dog walked straight into the big farm
kitchen and began poking her nose into cup-
boards and whining. The cat arched her
back, hissed and ran out into the yard.

'What on earth have you got there, Colin?' asked Mum who was ironing. 'We've got one already. Did you find old Charlie?'

'No,' said Colin. 'Mr Dixon came and he thinks the house is empty. He's going to phone the police. He told me to bring the dog home, and if ol' Charlie's gone away or something, I can keep her.'

'Oh can you?' said Mum. 'I don't know what your dad will say. However she's here now and you'd best feed her.'

She found a tin plate and Colin opened a tin of dog food and threw in a handful of dog biscuits. She trembled with excitement and wagged her tail furiously. She seemed to finish the meal in one great gulp and whined for more.

'That's enough for now,' said Mum. 'You've already fed her this afternoon. Give her some water and let her be.'

Colin sat down on the mat beside her. She laid her head on his lap and fell asleep. He stayed very still for a long time, fondling her ears and stroking her until Dad came in for a drink and a last cheese sandwich before Colin's bedtime. Joy joined them, grumbling about her homework, but they mostly talked about Old Charlie and the sleeping dog.

'Dad, if he's gone away or dead or something, can I keep her?'

'That's not fair,' said Joy. 'She ought to belong to both of us. She's littler than Growler and not nearly so fierce. I like her.'

But Colin shook his head. 'If you want another dog, you get one for yourself,' he said. 'This one's mine; just mine.'

'Bedtime, Colin,' said Mum quickly, fearing a quarrel. 'Mind you wash properly and don't you be too sure about that dog. Old Charlie may be there all the time and anyhow your Dad hasn't said you could keep her.'

Dad's mouth was full but he looked straight at Colin and Colin looked straight at Dad. Dad winked; Colin hugged him and went up to bed.

But not to sleep. Dad had to be up milking at half past four and he and Mum went to bed soon after Colin. Colin waited until he heard them come upstairs and shut their bedroom door. Joy was in her room, finishing her homework.

Colin crept downstairs on silent bare feet and the dog whined, lifted her head and pawed his knees. 'You're lonely in this strange place,' whispered Colin. 'You can come and sleep with me tonight.'

And when Mum went to wake Colin for school next morning, she nearly exploded with rage. Colin lay fast asleep with his head on the pillow and, snuggled up against him with *her* head on the pillow, lay the dog.

Chapter three

When Colin came out of school next day, the vicar was waiting for him and walked down the road with him.

'Well?' said Mr Dixon. 'What about that dog?'

'She's fine. Dad says I can keep her. What about ol' Charlie?'

'We've found out about him. The police got in and found the house empty. But there was a letter from his sister in Ledbury and they phoned her. Charlie went on the bus to spend the day with her last Saturday and was taken ill and rushed into hospital. He didn't know anything till last night, but now he's coming round and asking about the dog. I said not to worry, she was in good hands.'

'That's right. But will ol' Charlie come home?'

'I doubt it; he's had what's called a stroke and his sister thinks he'll have to stay in hospital. If he hears the dog's in a good home, I think he'll be glad to leave it at that.'

Colin stood still in the middle of the road and looked at the vicar. 'Then she's mine?' he asked.

'Seems like it,' said the vicar.

'Then you tell ol' Charlie she'll have a good home all right,' said Colin. 'I'd best get back and see how she's doing. Can I bring her to Boys' Club?'

'Er . . . I suppose so,' said the vicar rather doubtfully. 'As long as they don't all want to bring dogs. We'll see how it goes.'

'Thanks,' said Colin and set off up the lane as fast as his legs would carry him. He reached the farm very out of breath and met his dad going across to the milking.

'She's mine, Dad,' he puffed, 'mine to keep.'

'What is?'

'The dog. Ol' Charlie's in hospital and probably not coming back. I can keep her; you did say I could, didn't you, Dad?'

'Well, I suppose so; but she's to sleep in the kitchen and that's that. Understand? Your mum was real vexed finding her all wound up in the clean sheets like that.'

Colin grinned, and ran to the house. The dog came barking to meet him. He flung his arms round her neck. 'You're mine and I'm going to call you Friska,' he whispered. 'I'll let Joy take you out for a walk sometimes but you're mine, mine, mine.'

28

Poor Joy didn't get much of a chance because Friska would follow no one but Colin. The dog howled when Colin went to school and rushed down the lane to meet him on his return home. On Saturday he walked her far across the fields and woods and on Sunday he wanted to take her to church.

'The vicar wouldn't mind,' said Colin. 'She was ever so good at Boys' Club.'

'Don't be daft Colin,' said Mum. Friska started whining and Joy started laughing. 'You'll have her in the choir with me next,' she said.

'Now come on, come on and stop fooling,' said Dad, suddenly appearing in his Sunday suit and tie. They set off down the lane and when they reached the road the bell was tolling fast. Joy ran ahead to dress for the choir.

Everyone in the village liked the vicar and

the church was nearly full for the Family Service. Colin enjoyed the first part when the children sang or read, and the hymns, but he did not often listen to the sermon unless the vicar was telling a story. That day the vicar read a verse from the Bible twice through and then made the children say it after him:–

'The Lord says, "Do not fear, I have redeemed you. I have called you by name; you are Mine." '

And then – Colin could hardly believe it; the vicar did not actually say his name but he was talking about him.

'This week,' said Mr Dixon, 'rather a sad thing happened to old Mr Brown who lived on the edge of the common. But it would have been much sadder if it had not been for two kind, sensible boys.'

Colin blushed all over.

The vicar went on to talk about the

hungry, lonely dog and how two boys had noticed and cared (Colin turned his head and giggled at Bill). He told how he and Colin had whistled at the gate and how the dog had come rushing out and how Colin had said, 'Then she's mine now; she'll have a good home all right.'

He went on to say how the dog had come to Boys' Club but would go to no one but her own master. 'He's named her Friska,' said the vicar, 'he only has to call her name and the dog runs to him. She isn't lonely or hungry or frightened any more. She's his, and I know he'll care for her.'

Colin grinned at Dad and nudged Mum.

'And it was this,' said the vicar, 'that reminded me of this verse in the Bible.' He went on to explain that God called people to come to him, and they could either say no or answer his call, like Friska, and belong to a master who would love them and care for them; who would say to them, 'Don't be afraid, I have redeemed you; I have called you by your name. If you answer and come to me, you will be mine for ever, and safe for ever.'

There was more, but Colin was so excited that he didn't listen much to the rest of it. When it was over, Joy came running to him, looking quite proud of him. 'Fancy having a sermon all about you, Colin,' she said very loudly and the people near looked at him and laughed. The grocer said, 'Well done, lad!' and his teacher said, 'So you were the hero of the story, were you?' and

Colin went pinker than ever. But he did not linger long, for, up at the farm, his dog was waiting for him. He left Mum and Dad and Joy talking outside the church and hurried up the lane.

But as he ran, part of that verse kept going round and round in his head and he wanted to get home and say it to Friska. 'Don't be afraid; I have called you by your name. You are mine.'

Chapter four

Old Charlie never came back; he went to live in a home for old people near to his sister and Friska stayed at the farm. Colin could hardly remember the time when Friska hadn't been there, waiting for him at the bottom of the stairs in the morning, seeing him off to school, scampering down the lane to meet him on his return, all ready for a run. She was a beautiful, glossy, bright-eyed dog now and so well-behaved that no one at the farm was sorry that they had taken her in.

The summer holidays came and Colin helped with the hay, swam in the river and wandered over the countryside with Bill and Friska. At the beginning of August the boys went to camp and Joy promised to look after Friska. It was a glorious week but, when the last day came, Colin could hardly wait to get back to his dog and was nearly knocked over by her welcome.

September came and it was time to go back to school. The leaves were beginning to turn yellow and the hills were hidden by mists in the morning. The plums and apples were ripening in the orchard and one Saturday afternoon, Joy and Colin decided to go blackberrying.

'If you go down toward the hopyards they'll be best,' said Mum. 'They ripen quicker down in the valley.'

The children ran down the rutted track

that led to the distant hop fields on the
further side of the farm. To the left lay
the orchards but, on the right, the woods
came down to the track and the hedges were
heavy with blackberries. Joy and Colin
picked fast and Friska ran into the woods
to hunt for rabbits.

Suddenly they heard a furious barking and Colin, spilling half his berries, dashed in among the trees. He saw Friska dart forward, as though to attack an enormous Alsatian who was straining to reach her and growling in his deep throat. Colin seized Friska's collar just in time and was glad to see that the other dog was also firmly held, by two boys a little older than himself. They wore bright, rather ragged clothes and one carried a sack over his back. Neither they nor the dog looked very friendly and Colin felt rather scared. He made for the edge of the wood, dragging Friska behind him, still barking.

Joy had climbed the bank to see what was going on and, being as big as they were, she wasn't at all afraid. She smiled at the strange boys, asked them what they had got in their sack and offered them a biscuit each from their picnic. The boys were pleased.

The big dog had a biscuit too and stopped growling. Friska stopped barking and Colin stopped feeling afraid.

'Want to see?' said the older boy. He opened the sack and pulled out a pink-eyed, yellow-toothed ferret with dirty white fur. He pushed it toward Joy. 'Introduce you to Percy,' he said.

Joy backed. 'Ugh!' she said. 'You've been rabbiting, haven't you. How many did you catch?'

'Only two. Swagger's not much good at rabbiting; he's too big. That's a nice looking little dog you've got there. Want to sell 'im?'

'Not on your life,' said Colin quickly. It was such a terrible idea that he put his arms round Friska and held her tight.

'Where d'you live?' asked the big lad.

'Up at the farm on the hill. Where do you?'

'In a better house than yours. Want to see?'

'Yes; how far?'

'Just down by the road in the lay-by. Want to come?'

Joy and Colin looked at each other. Colin gave a little nod.

'Come on then,' said Joy, 'show us. It'll soon be sunset so we mustn't be long.'

They ran down the track until they came to the main road. A van was parked in the lay-by hitched to a trailer – a long, white caravan with scarlet curtains. A group of people sat round eating a meal. The children stopped a little way off.

'There,' said the older boy proudly. 'Good, isn't it. These are my folks. His folks live in another trailer. It'll be along soon.'

'It's lovely,' said Joy. 'I wish I lived in a house like that. Where are you going?'

'Dunno; on to the hops somewhere. Might be anywhere. Want to see inside?'

'Not now, we must go back. Mum'll tell us off if we're not home before dark. But one day, if you like, you can come and see us at the farm.'

'Thanks,' said the older boy. 'I'll do that. So long!' He smiled in a friendly way but the younger boy said nothing at all. He just stared and his bright, black eyes were fixed on Friska.

Joy and Colin hurried up the track, talking about the caravan. They thought it must be wonderful to live in a trailer, always moving on. The farm seemed quite dull. It was getting dusk and rabbits were coming out in the twilight. Friska kept rushing into the woods and the children did not wait for her. She often chased rabbits and she knew her way home.

They arrived back happy and hungry with scratched hands and scarlet lips. Mum was baking and there was a lovely smell in the kitchen. Joy and Colin settled down on the hearthrug with mugs of tea and told Mum all about their adventure and how they wished they lived in a caravan. Mum laughed and said, give her the farm any day.

'Friska's late,' said Colin suddenly. 'I wonder if she's caught a rabbit for a change. She hardly ever does. She makes too much noise.'

'Let her be,' said Mum. 'A dog wants to run and rabbit and have a bit of fun on its own. She'll come in her own time.'

Colin went to the door and stood looking out at the darkening hills. A new moon hung behind the woods and an owl hooted. He felt rather jealous of Friska having fun on her own without him. He whistled.

There was no answer; the owl hooted again. Colin stepped out into the yard and looked round. Friska must be having a very exciting time to make her stay out so long. He walked a little way to where the woods came down to the edge of the path.

'Friska,' he called. 'Good dog! Come home now. Good dog!'

But there was still no answer. The leaves rustled and some little animals stirred in the ditch; just the ordinary night sounds. No happy barking or scampering paws. Colin suddenly felt very frightened and rushed back to the house. He was glad to find his father in the kitchen.

'Dad! Mum! Joy!' he shouted. 'Friska's

not there! She never goes far. She always comes when I call. She's gone!'

'Let's all call,' said Joy, and they all ran outside. Up and down the path they went, calling, calling. They went all the way back to the place where they had picked blackberries and then all the way back home, calling till they were hoarse. But it was no good. Friska had completely disappeared.

'We'll have to go home now, Colin,' said Dad sadly. 'Maybe someone's stolen her. We'll get the police on to it in the morning.'

They went back into the kitchen and Dad leaned back in the armchair and took his poor, sobbing little boy into his arms. 'We'll find her, son,' he said. 'Maybe she'll come home in the night. We'll sleep with the doors open and we'll hear if she scratches.'

Joy looked up suddenly. 'Col,' she said, 'do you think that boy could have taken her? He wanted to buy her and he kept looking at her.'

Colin gave a big sniff and sat up.

'But she was with us till we were nearly home,' he said. 'I saw her chase a rabbit into the woods just below the crab apple tree.'

'He could have followed us,' said Joy. 'It was getting dark and we were hurrying. We didn't look round.'

Colin got quite excited. 'Then the police could find him,' he said. 'We know what the caravan looks like, white with red curtains. I'd know it anywhere.'

Joy shook her head. 'That one belonged to the big boy's family,' she said. 'The other one was waiting for the trailer to arrive. We didn't see it. But we'd know Friska anywhere. It ought to be easy.'

'We'll get the police on to it first thing tomorrow morning,' said Dad comfortably.

'Now how about a cup of tea, Mother, and then bed?'

Colin drank his cup of tea and went up to bed very quietly. His mother looked in later and thought he was asleep. His father only discovered their mistake next morning when he came downstairs, yawning, to the five o'clock milking and found the sofa pulled across by the door and his son curled up under a rug.

Colin was taking no risks.

Chapter five

It was a sad rainy morning and Colin came in late to breakfast, cold and wet and very miserable. He had been up early, searching the woods. He thought perhaps Friska had caught her paw in a poacher's trap, but Dad shook his head.

'We'd have heard her howling a mile away,' he said. 'I think Joy's right and she's gone with the hop pickers. I'll ring the police after breakfast.'

But the police were not very hopeful. The

hop fields were spread out all over the county and Colin hadn't seen the right trailer. They had to have a warrant to search caravans. Every caravan had one or two dogs and their owners all vowed they'd had them from birth. Stolen dogs were usually tied up inside the vans and only let out at night. Still, they'd have a look round.

'Well,' said Mum, 'we'd best get ready for church. Tidy your hair, Joy. Don't forget your tie, Dad! Colin, if you'd rather stop home, you can do so. I don't suppose the dog will come but you never know.'

Colin hesitated. He somehow felt that he would like to see the vicar, who'd been really helpful over tracking down old Charlie and who always seemed to have good ideas when things went wrong. But, on the other hand, if Friska came home, Colin certainly did not want her to come home to an empty house. He decided to stay. 'But tell the vicar why,' he said. 'He'll want to know about Friska.'

But there was no sign of Friska and Colin wandered about the yard or sat in the kitchen window and the time seemed very long indeed. He thought it must be long past dinner time but the clock in the hall told him he was wrong, although they were certainly rather late. At last he heard Joy clatter up the steps and fling open the door.

'The vicar's coming, Col,' she announced breathlessly. 'He's coming specially to see you.'

51

Colin ran to the window. Sure enough, Mum, Dad and the vicar were coming across the yard and the vicar had changed from his church clothes into an old jacket and Wellington boots. Colin jumped the steps and met him. 'Did they tell you?' he said. 'She's gone. Dad thinks it might be the hop pickers, but it might be a trap . . .'

'Well, if it might be a trap, let's have one more search round,' said the vicar. 'There's an hour to lunch and the sun's coming out. Look, there's a rainbow over the hills. Have you been round to old Charlie's place?'

'Have a cupper before you go,' said Mum bustling in with a tray laid with cups, creamy farm milk and home made rock buns. The teapot followed in a few minutes. They all sat round the kitchen table together and Colin felt a little more cheerful. Outside, the rainbow grew brighter and brighter and all the world looked clean and shining.

'Come on,' said the vicar, when he had drunk two cups of tea and eaten two rock cakes. 'Let's be off.'

They searched the woods right up to the ridge and down the other side. They went across to Charlie's house which was a wilderness of weeds and nettles. It was nearly dinner time and they sat down on the rough log outside the window. Colin was quite tired and very miserable again.

'Supposing Friska's caught in a trap,' he said. 'Or supposing she's gone with that boy. Perhaps she's hungry or perhaps he'll beat her. And she won't like being shut in a caravan. Friska's an outdoor dog.'

'Migrant workers are usually kind to their animals,' said the vicar. 'But, Colin, do you ever pray about things?'

Colin nodded. 'I say my prayers at night,' he said. 'I say, "Our Father which art in Heaven" and then I say, "bless Mum and Dad and Joy and me," and last night I said, "bless Friska." '

'Well, that's a good prayer. But do you ever think that there really is a Father in Heaven and you can belong to him and tell him everything and ask him to help you?'

Colin shook his head slowly. He had never really thought about it like that.

'Well, it's a good thing to know. It makes things all different. Do you remember the verse you learned that Sunday when I told the story of you and your dog?'

Colin smiled. ' "Don't be afraid." I can't remember the middle bit. "I have called you by your name; you are mine." I said it to Friska when I got home.'

The vicar laughed. '*You* said it to *Friska*, but *God* says it to *you*. "Don't be afraid, Colin. I have redeemed you. I have called you by your name; you are mine." '

'What does redeem mean?' asked Colin.

'It means to buy back. It means that God loves us and wants us to belong to him. But sometimes we listen to Satan and go the wrong way and do wrong things and Satan says, "You are mine now." But Jesus came and took all those wrong things on himself when he died on the cross. He paid for them; he bought us back. Now he calls us to be his, and you can say yes or no.'

'Best say yes,' said Colin.

'Yes, much better say yes, because when you belong to God, then you have a loving Heavenly Father and you can tell him everything. You can tell him about Friska and ask him to help you find her. He doesn't always give us exactly what we ask for, but he loves to help and he always does the thing that is right and best.'

'It would be right and best to find Friska,' said Colin. 'Could you ask him now?'

So they prayed and asked God to look after Friska wherever she was and to bring her back. Then they left the cottage and said goodbye. Mr Dixon went down the hill and Colin went up the hill feeling much happier. If God was really so great, he must know where Friska was and he would look after her.

Chapter six

The week passed slowly and sadly. The police said they were still keeping their eyes open but, so far, they had seen nothing of a black mongrel dog. Every day Colin hurried back from school with just a tiny hope in his heart that Friska might come rushing down the lane yapping a welcome. But there was no sound except the cows, mooing as they went to the milking, or Growler's deep bark and the rattle of his chain. Growler was a big, fierce watch dog who guarded the yard but he was a comfort just then. He would put his huge paws on Colin's shoulders and lick his face and pretend to be a gentle dog. Colin would sometimes weep a few tears into his bristly coat and bring him stale buns and bread when Dad wasn't looking.

And then it was Saturday morning again and Colin woke very early. Dad was in the barn and the house was quite silent. It was a clear day with golden leaves blowing about and sprays of crimson creeper waving in the wind. Colin leaned on the sill and suddenly knew what he was going to do that day. He would have one last try. After all, Friska must be somewhere and he was nearly always allowed to do what he liked on Saturday. He thought of waking Joy and asking her to go with him but then he remembered she had to go back to school for a hockey match.

He dressed and went to the larder and found some food; two cold sausages, some pork pie, bread and butter and a slice of apple tart. He put on his strongest shoes and his anorak with a big pocket. He was ready to set off and no one must stop him. He wouldn't even tell Dad in case he tried to talk him out of it. He'd just write a note to Mum and go.

So he started off down the track, past the crab apple tree and the orchards, past the blackberry hedges till he came to the road and the lay-by where the van and its trailer had parked. It had been heading north toward Worcester and there were hop yards all the way. He would pretend he was a policeman keeping his eyes open for a black mongrel dog. It would be fun and, who knows? He might have better luck than the police.

He trotted along for hours and the warm September sun rose high in the sky. He was going along a country road between hedges fluffy with old man's beard and bright with hips and haws and bryony berries. He kept stopping to eat blackberries and did not go very fast. Behind the hedges the hop yards stretched away as far as he could see but there were no caravans; only, now and again, clusters of sheds where the pickers from Birmingham bedded down. Colin went as close to these as he dared and watched for a long time. But they were mostly locked and deserted, for the people were all out working in the fields and there were no dogs about.

He began to get very tired and sat down under a tree to eat his lunch, keeping back a sausage sandwich, in case he found Friska.

The sun was almost overhead now and he knew that he would soon come to a village, because he had sometimes driven there with his Dad, and he also knew that there was a shop. He felt very thirsty and was delighted to find that he had 30p in his anorak pocket. He could buy some Coke.

The village came in sight at last and he trailed into the shop looking hot and dusty. The shopkeeper was a kind woman and let him sit on an empty bottle case to drink his Coke. He bought a sherbert fountain and two lollipops with the change. Being nearly dinner time, the shop was almost empty and both Colin and the woman were inclined to be chatty. Colin told her all about Friska and asked her whether she knew of any caravans parked near the village.

'Well, there's three or four parked on the common through the village,' she said. 'But you be careful, my lad. What do you think you're going to do if you see your dog?'

'I'll call her by her name,' said Colin.
'She'll come to me at once.'

'And maybe there's others as will come
after you at once,' said the woman. 'Don't
you do any such thing! If you see your
dog, you go straight home and call your
dad. Your mum oughtn't to have let you
come all this way alone, and you just a kid.'

'She didn't know,' said Colin. 'Are hop
pickers fierce?'

'There's good and bad, much the same as

other folks. Some are really nice, some are really rough. But they won't take kindly to you walking off with what they think is their dog. Now it's one o'clock and I must shut shop and give my hubby his lunch. If you run up against any trouble, you come right back here.'

Colin set off past the cottages and oast houses and walked until he could see the vans and trailers on the common. There was quite a group of them, one behind the other. He moved a little nearer and then stopped short. The last caravan but one was long and white and had scarlet curtains and Colin knew it at once; and there was another caravan parked just beyond it and the pickers, who had come in for their lunch, were sitting round on steps and benches drinking from mugs and smoking their pipes; and right in the middle of the group lay a large Alsatian dog.

Chapter seven

There was an old stone wall at the edge of the common and Colin crouched behind it. He could not see much but he knew that he would have to wait. This was the pickers' lunch hour but later, he supposed, they would go back to the fields, leaving the big Alsatian to guard the camp. One thing, however, he had noticed; the animal was chained.

If he could creep round to the back of the last caravan without the dog seeing him, he

67

could at least whisper at the keyhole. If
the boys had travelled together they had
probably camped together, or perhaps
Friska was in one of the nearer caravans.
But if she was there, he would only have to
whisper. She would know his voice at once.
He wasn't sure what he would do after
that. He would have to wait and see.

He waited for a long time and he felt
very small and alone. Big clouds massed up,

hiding the sun. Now and again he stood up and peered round the wall. The men had gone back, one by one, to the fields, and at last only one old woman remained, nursing a baby; and the big Alsatian dog.

And now his moment had come; he felt very frightened. If only he hadn't come alone; if only Dad or the vicar or even Joy were with him. He remembered that Sunday morning when he and the vicar had searched the woods and sat on the bench outside old Charlie's cottage. It had been a shining morning and earlier on there had been a great rainbow. He stood still, remembering what they had talked about. 'Don't be afraid ... then the word that meant to buy back ... I have called you by your name; you are mine.'

He tried to remember what Mr Dixon had said about it ... the Father in Heaven calling us to be his children ... we could say yes or no . . . then we were his and we need never feel lonely or afraid. He would always be there loving us, helping us.

'My name's Colin,' he whispered, 'and I'm saying yes. I want to be yours. Please help me now and don't let me be so frightened.'

It was very quiet; the sun shone out suddenly from behind a grey cloud. Up in a mountain ash tree, scarlet against the orange berries, a robin sang and sang. The sun made everything look bright and the robin's song was clear and brave and happy. 'Perhaps that's God answering me,' thought Colin. 'I'll go ahead.'

He tiptoed across the common, away from the camp, until he was hidden out of sight behind the vans and trailers at the far end. Then he turned round and began tiptoeing toward them. The old woman and the dog were hidden by the last two caravans. They could not see Colin and he could not see them.

When he reached the shelter of the last caravan he crouched down and waited again for a long time, listening with his ear against the wall. Once or twice he thought he heard a scuffling movement inside. If Friska was there, he was surprised that she could not hear the loud beating of his heart.

Then he took a deep breath and did it. Creeping round the corner of the caravan, he stood on tiptoe against the steps and put his mouth to the crack below the door.

'Friska,' he called, as loudly as he dared, 'Friska, good dog, it's me, Colin. . . .'

He got no further; it sounded as though

something had suddenly exploded inside the caravan. There was a mad rush of paws, a frantic barking, a sound of furniture being knocked over, the hurtling of a body against the door. And, at the same time, the big Alsatian began barking too, straining at his lead, and the old woman came hobbling across the grass, calling out. A man appeared in the gap that led to the hopyards, shouting, and Colin doubled up and ran as he had never run before, dodging from caravan to caravan, streaking across the common and back to the wall. But if they ran after him, they would find him behind the wall; he must go further. Doubling up again he ran uphill to where a beech tree grew with spreading roots and low boughs. It seemed made for him. He jumped, scrambled and started climbing, hand over hand, high up into the shelter of the thinner branches where no Alsatian could reach him. He snuggled against the trunk until he got his breath back, and then peeped out through the veil of golden leaves.

Everything was spread out below him; he could see the yellow bracken on the common and the hop poles stretching away toward the sky. Just below him was the cluster of vans and trailers and blue smoke rising from a bonfire and people moving about. Behind him he could see the roofs and chimneys of the village and the white road winding home. Everything was quiet again, and there was no sign of the big Alsatian. He breathed a great sigh of relief, rested his cheek against the smooth bark and closed his eyes. He felt very safe and very happy. Friska was there, in the last caravan, and Dad or the police would find her.

But when he opened his eyes, he noticed something else. The shadows were growing long and the sun was beginning to sink toward his home hills. The days were getting shorter; he had been out a very long time and he had better get moving. He shinned down the tree but he did not dare appear on the road. He crept along behind brambles and gorse bushes until the village was well in sight. Then he ran to the shop.

The lady at the counter looked up in

surprise as the little boy with scratched hands and dirty face walked in. There were several people in the shop and Colin sat down on the wooden case and waited his turn. At last she was free, and turned to him.

'Well,' she asked, 'what happened?'

Colin looked up with a big grin. 'Found her!' he said. 'At least, I know where she is.'

'Good for you. What are you going to do now?'

'Fetch my dad; could I phone him?'

'Sure; know his number?'

Colin nodded. Mum answered the phone and when she heard his voice she sounded very cross indeed and almost crying.

'Where *are* you, Colin?' she cried. 'Your dad's been searching the county for you. He's been asking at all the camps and nobody had seen you. He's just about to call the police. How could you do such a thing?'

Colin was quite surprised. 'But I told you, Mum,' he said, 'I was going to look for Friska; and, Mum, I've found her!'

'Found her?'

'Yes, but I haven't got her yet. I'm in the village shop at Leigh. Tell Dad to come at once; it's very important.'

'I told you, he was out looking for you, but he keeps phoning the house in case you turn up. Just stop where you are, Colin, and your dad'll come.'

So Colin stopped and the lady gave him crisps and pop and a stale sugar bun, even though he hadn't any money left; and he sat watching through the window and talking about Friska when there were no customers, until just before closing time, the old farm van rattled up and Dad burst into the shop.

'Where's the lad?' he asked breathlessly, looking round. Then he saw Colin sitting on the box.

'Don't you ever do a thing like that again, Colin,' said Dad quite angrily. 'Scared the life out of your Mum, you did. Now what's all this about the dog? Mum said you'd found her.'

Colin nodded. He wasn't at all frightened. He could see from Dad's face that he was really rather proud of him.

'She's in the last caravan on the common,' he said. 'You've got to come and get her with me but you'll have to be careful of the big Alsatian.'

He got up and thanked the lady very politely and promised to bring Friska to visit her another day. Then he slipped his hand into his father's.

'Come on, Dad,' he said. 'Friska will think I've gone away and forgotten her.'

Chapter eight

They got into the van and drove straight to the camp. Dad parked on the common and he and Colin walked toward the caravans. The light was beginning to fade and the hop pickers were coming from the yards. Iron pots bubbled over primuses and bonfires and the delicious smell of rabbit or pheasant stew hung over the air. A large strong man was working on the last van and his arms were covered with grease and motor oil; but

Dad was large and strong too and he went up to him.

'Evening, mate,' he said pleasantly. 'There seems to have been a bit of a mix-up. I believe you've got my lad's dog in the trailer. Can we have a look? It's a black mongrel bitch.'

The man looked Dad full in the face. 'You see our dog,' he said, pointing to the large Alsatian. 'He's the only one we've got; and if I let him off the chain you'd best run for it. Fierce as a wolf, he is. Eat your lad up in two mouthfuls if I told him to.'

They stood facing each other. Colin, still holding his dad's hand, felt a little push and he understood. He darted to the steps and called at the top of his voice. 'Friska!' he yelled, 'It's Colin. Good dog, Friska, good dog.'

Once again there was a sudden explosion and the caravan seemed to rock. Friska was

80

hurling herself against the door over and over again, barking and howling madly, scratching with all her might. The Alsatian also strained at its lead and barked furiously and a crowd of pickers came running up from round the bonfires. A woman's shrill voice cried, 'Let the beast out, can't you, before she smashes all the china.'

A boy ran forward and opened the door and Friska sprang out with a force that made the crowd fall backwards. 'Friska!'

shouted Colin again and she turned and leaped on him, knocking him down and they rolled on the grass together, laughing and barking. Then Colin got up and Friska stood on her hind legs, put her paws on her master's shoulders, licked his face and wagged her tail.

Another boy ran forward. 'Rover,' he called loudly. 'Rover, come here.'

Colin glanced at him. It was beginning to get dark, but Colin thought that he recognised him. Friska took not the slightest notice. Then she turned and growled at the man who had been looking on in silence. He suddenly chuckled.

'Rover,' he said. 'Rover indeed! You wait till I get my hands on you, son.'

The farmer stepped forward. 'Look, mate,' he said. 'We don't want the police in on this; there's another fortnight of picking and you won't want to shift yet. My lad's

been breaking his heart over that dog this week past. Maybe yours thought she was lost, maybe not, but I'm willing to make it good to him. Take this and let's be going and good luck to you.'

The man held out his hand and there was a rustle of money. 'Thanks,' he said, 'and good luck to you and your lad.'

Dad and Colin walked back to the van

with Friska bounding beside them. They
drove through the village in silence because
Colin was almost too happy to speak. Then
as they sped up the white country road that
led home, Colin leaned over the back of the
seat and said, 'Dad, did you pay to get her
back?'

'Why, yes,' said Dad. 'She's a good dog
and worth it.' He rumpled Colin's hair.
'Taking you all round, you're not a bad lad
either.'

'But she was ours already; why should we pay for her?'

'Well, finding's keeping round here, and I didn't want a fuss, not with that crowd. Besides, she got away; but you must keep an eye on her in future, Col, specially at hopping time.'

They were silent again. Now they could see the farm on the hill ahead of them, black against the last glow, and the warm light streaming from the kitchen window. Colin was longing to tell Dad all about his great day, but he was saving it up till they were all together.

'Dad,' he said suddenly, 'It's like the second part of the verse, the bit I always forget; it says, don't be afraid, I've bought you back.'

'What verse?' said Dad. Don't know what you mean . . . and if your mum's vexed, Colin, remember you deserve it. You never ought to have gone off on your own like that, scaring her stiff.'

But although Mum had meant to scold, she was too pleased to see Friska and, when she heard the story, so proud of Colin that she forgot all about it. And Colin was so tired he only just managed to tell it and to swallow his favourite supper of sausages, chips and green peas before dropping asleep. He wanted to go to sleep because he wanted to wake up in the morning and find Friska in her basket by the stove.

He was up early next day and he and Friska ran out into the cool, misty morning. The grass was covered with spiders' webs and they went down across the fields and picked some mushrooms for breakfast. Colin always took Friska for a run on Sunday morning because she had to stay behind when they went to church. He specially wanted to go to church that

morning because he wanted to tell the vicar all about his great adventure, and the moment the service was over, Colin rushed up to him.

'Hey, Mr Dixon,' he said, seizing his sleeve, 'you know Friska who was lost, well, I went and found her. I went all by myself all the way to Leigh and I saw the caravans and ...'

'Just a moment,' said the vicar. 'This is too good to hurry. I'll go and shake hands with the people and you ask your mum if you can come over to the vicarage with me. My wife will fix some elevenses and you can tell me all about it.'

So Joy promised to tell Friska that Colin wouldn't be long and, about twenty minutes later, Colin and the vicar sat down to a tray of hot cocoa and ginger biscuits in the vicarage sitting room and the vicar's wife and baby came in to listen too. And when Colin had finished his exciting story, he said, 'And you know, Vicar, it was like the second bit of that verse, the bit I forget; Dad bought him back, and when I was sitting behind the wall I was ever so frightened and I said yes.'

The vicar blinked. 'I don't quite understand,' he said.

'Well, you said that when we feel frightened, God calls us by our name and we can say yes or no, and I said yes, and it was like as though God said, "You are mine." And then I wasn't so frightened any more. And Friska wasn't frightened when I called her by her name; she came bounding out and then she was mine again, but Dad had to pay for her like you said.'

'Yes,' said the vicar gently, 'you've remembered very well. "Don't be afraid; I have redeemed you," which means, I have

bought you back. And you had to be bought back too, Colin, before you could belong to God. Just like Friska got into the wrong hands, so we follow Satan. We tell lies and are selfish and lose our tempers and Satan says, "You are mine," and you can never belong to God or go into his home. After all, if lies and quarrelling went into heaven, it wouldn't be heaven any longer, would it?'

Colin looked thoughtful. He had often quarrelled and sometimes told lies.

'So Jesus came. He died on the cross and was punished instead of us for the wrong things we had done. He paid for them instead of us so now we can be forgiven and belong to God again. That is what redeemed means. That's why we love him so much; because he loved us enough to suffer so much.'

Colin listened and nodded his head. He

had to get back to Friska but he understood what that verse meant now. "Don't be afraid; I have redeemed you. I have called you by your name; you are mine." God said it to him and he could say it to Friska. He thought about it as he walked up the lane, scuffling through the golden leaves that had already started to fall, and he felt very happy. Friska would always love him for walking all that way and braving the big

Alsatian and creeping up to the caravan and calling her by her name, but Jesus had done far more. He had died on the cross and suffered a lot of pain to redeem Colin.

'I love him too,' thought Colin. 'I'm glad I said yes; I'm glad I belong to God.' There was a wild barking and Friska came hurtling down the lane to meet him. 'And I am so very, very glad that Friska is home again.'

More exciting books to enjoy in the *Read by Myself* series...

Meep comes to earth

Heather Butler

"Wonder whose ideas Mr Bradbury has decided to use for the school play..." said Billy.

Mr Bradbury announced, "It's been very difficult choosing which play to put on. You all came up with such wonderful ideas. I eventually decided that Robert and Billy's play about the robot was the best. It has lots of action and a good beginning, middle..." "and end!" everyone joined in.

ISBN 1 85999 320 6
Price £3.50

Other Titles by Patricia St John

The Tanglewoods' Secret

Ruth was only good at getting into trouble and planning outrageous schemes. There seemed to be no end to her mischief until the day she actually ran away.

ISBN 1 85999 267 6
Price £3.99

Treasures of the Snow

Annette knew she could never forgive Lucien, and she was going to make sure that no one else did either. But then some surprising things began to happen to both of them.

ISBN 1 85999 266 8
Price £3.99

Available from your local Christian bookshop

Mystery of Pheasant Cottage
Lucy's quiet home at Pheasant Cottage is shrouded in mystery – she is determined at all costs to find out what is being hidden from her.
ISBN 1 85999 512 8 £3.50

Rainbow Garden
For Elaine, packed off to Wales from London, it's only the little garden she finds at the end of the rainbow that makes her stay worthwhile.
ISBN 1 85999 510 1 £3.99

The Secret of the Fourth Candle
Three exciting stories set in North Africa where Patricia St John worked as a missionary.
ISBN 1 85999 511 X £3.50

Star of Light
When Si Mohammed tries to sell his little blind step-daughter to a beggar, Hamid sets out to rescue her.
ISBN 0 85421 883 1 £3.50

Available from you local Christian bookshop, online at www.scriptureunion.org.uk/publishing or call Mail Order direct on 01908 856006.